This book was given to you by someone who cares about you and your tomorrows…

ALL THE BEST TO YOU ALWAYS.

Baba Ganoush

INTRODUCTION

Thank you for your interest in "Little Lessons, Wisdom and Truth" Volume I. The intention is to help pass life lessons on to the little ones in our lives through short illustrated stories.

Parenting, Grandparenting, Aunting, Uncleing and teaching are huge responsibilities. If "Little Lessons, Wisdom & Truth" helps to point youngsters in the right direction, it's done what it was designed to do.

If you like the book and feel it would have value to others, please refer them to the place you purchased it and also consider purchasing a copy for the schools, library, book club, reading group, YMCA or place of worship you are affiliated with.

All the best to you as you confront the daunting, yet rewarding task of raising or helping to raise the next generation that will shape and hopefully have a positive impact on our world. May your efforts produce creative, solid young people of character and integrity.

Please look for the LLW&T ebook as well as a coloring book version to be available in the future.

Edition – 10.25.2018

2

Don't forget to find "Little Baba" in each illustration.

Timmy Swimmy and his Mom were walking to the playground and Timmy was about to step on a grasshopper that had wandered onto the sidewalk. Mom saw what Timmy was about to do and said "Stop, think a second before you do that… Look closely at him. His little life is valuable to him and once you take it there's no getting it back, it's gone forever".

Timmy stopped and looked down at the grasshopper he had almost crushed… As he did, he found a new appreciation for the little creature and saw it for the unique living creation that it is.

As Timmy and his Mom walked away Timmy was glad to have stopped before he did something he couldn't take back…

Have respect for all living things… Even little creatures.

Timmy Swimmy got his balloon and was having a great time with his "new friend". They had been spending time together walking around the neighborhood enjoying a beautiful day.

A sudden breeze came up and before Timmy realized it, his balloon had slipped away and was rising into the heavens above. Timmy was very sad to have lost his balloon but as some time passed he wasn't quite as sad and began to think about his balloon a little bit differently.

Even though Timmy could no longer see his balloon he could take a little bit of comfort knowing his balloon still existed even though his friend had left his world for another one.

Things we care about may leave us at some point.

Timmy Swimmy and Brooksey Padooksey were playing next to each other at the water's edge. Timmy had a little shovel and Brooksey had a pail.

After playing for a while, Timmy noticed Brooksey had a pail. Timmy asked if he could borrow her pail and offered to lend her his shovel. Brooksey said, "Sure, let's see what we can build together." In just a little time they created the best sand castle either had made.

By sharing what each of them had, they were able to make something better than they could have made with just their own toys.

Sharing can make better things happen.

Timmy Swimmy and Bobby Robby were walking past the edge of a forest and saw a bird sitting on a branch singing. Bobby picked up a stone and said "I bet I can hit the bird on that branch".

Before Timmy could say or do anything the stone was on its way toward the little bird. The poor little bird didn't see the stone coming and it almost hit him… Fortunately, the stone missed and the little bird flew away scared but unhurt.

Timmy looked at Bobby and asked "do you believe in GOD"? Bobby said "Yes… Why?". Timmy said "GOD may have been watching and could have seen what you did".

GOD may be watching… Try not to let Him down.

Timmy Swimmy and Brooksey Padooksey were walking back from saying goodbye to their good friend Davey Wavey who was moving across town. They were both a little sad because they wouldn't see Davey as often.

Timmy remembered all of the stars he and Brooksey had seen last night on the way home. He thought about how he couldn't see them during the day even though he knew they were still there…

The next night Timmy and Brooksey took a walk and they could see the stars again. Timmy thought about how, like stars during the day, your good friends are still there even if you don't see them for a while, but like stars at night you will see them again.

Good friends are still there even when you don't see them.

Timmy Swimmy and Bobby Robby worked all summer for Mrs. Lilly Silly, a nice older lady who lived in their neighborhood. Each time they worked, they earned money for helping Mrs. Lilly with chores around her house.

Every time Timmy was paid he would go to the bank and save part of what he earned so he would have something to show for all his hard work. Bobby didn't think about saving any of the money he earned and spent everything he made.

Summer passed and Mrs. Lilly didn't need much help so Timmy and Bobby weren't able to make as much money. In the fall a new model of bike came out. Sadly, Bobby hadn't saved any money and couldn't buy one. Timmy, because he put money in the bank every time he was paid was able to buy himself the new bike. He also noticed the money he put in the bank had earned a little extra money the bank gave him called "interest".

It's important to save money... Especially when you're young so it has time to grow.

Timmy Swimmy's soccer coach Gerry Salsberry had the team gathered for a pregame talk. They were about to play the team with the best record in the league. Coach Gerry told them, "If each one of you can walk off the field after the game, look me in the eye and tell me you gave 100 percent that's all I and your teammates can ask. Now go out there, give it everything you've got and leave it all on the field".

Timmy and his teammates gave 100 percent and played as hard as they could. The game was close from the beginning to the end. Unfortunately, just before time ran out, the ball took a funny hop right to the other team's best player and he scored putting his team up by one goal and winning the game.

As the team walked off the field together, they were exhausted and not happy about losing… but they did feel good about how hard they played and giving 100 percent. Because they had done everything within their power to win, despite getting out scored, they could be happy about the way they played.

If you truly give 100 percent and did your best you've done all you can.

Timmy Swimmy and his friends were having a good time kicking the soccer ball around in his yard. Timmy's Mother enjoyed having Timmy's friends over and happened to be watching them play from the front door.

Bobby Robby was trying to pass the ball to Timmy but it was just a little over his head and went bouncing towards the street. Without thinking, Timmy ran chasing after the ball. He was about to run into the street to get the ball when he heard his mother yell "**STOP !!!**". Timmy stopped in his tracks, and as he did, a car whizzed past him…

It was a close call, but Timmy was ok because he listened to his parent quickly. As his Mom realized Timmy was safe she said "We can get a new ball, it's replaceable. We can NEVER get another you. You are irreplaceable… You ALWAYS have to look BOTH ways BEFORE going into the street. Sometimes you don't get a second chance to be careful. Please… be careful." Timmy knew she was right and was glad he had listened quickly.

Listening to your parents is important… really important.

AMERICAN HISTORY
END OF QUARTER
REPORT DUE IN JUST
TWO WEEKS!!!

Timmy Swimmy and Bobby Robby were in Mr. Listory's history class together. It was one of their favorite classes because Mr. Listory made history interesting by teaching WHY events occurred, not just when they happened. As the semester came to a close, Mr. Listory gave the class two weeks to complete their end of quarter report.

Timmy started doing a little work on his report each day even though it meant he couldn't play after school quite as long as he wanted. He knew by starting early he would avoid the stress of rushing at the last minute. Bobby kept letting days go by without doing any work on his report…
As the report's due date approached, the Spring Fair Timmy and Bobby had really looked forward to going to opened.

For months they talked about how much fun the rides and games would be. On opening day, Timmy went by Bobby's to get him to go to the fair. Unfortunately, Bobby had to tell Timmy he couldn't go because he only had one day to do his entire report. Because Timmy had worked hard on his report early, the pressure was off and he was able to have a fun relaxing day at the fair knowing he had finished his report ahead of time.

What you do today determines how difficult tomorrow will be.

Timmy Swimmy, Bobby Robby and their friends were playing baseball at the local park. Brooksey Padooksey also brought her dog Wolffy down to the park to watch the game. It was a close game and both teams wanted to win. Timmy hit a ball that looked like it was going to be a base hit.

Suddenly, Wolffy dog ran onto the field and grabbed the ball… Both teams began to argue that the play was going to go their way before Wolffy dog grabbed the ball. However, there was no way to tell. After several minutes neither team was willing to give in. Timmy thought for a minute and asked the other team, "What's fair since we can't tell what would have happened ?".

The other team agreed there was no way to tell what would have happened. Timmy said "Why don't we have a do over, that way it's fair to both teams ?". Everyone agreed that made sense and was the fairest solution. Timmy went back to the plate and everyone else went back to where they were before Wolffy dog grabbed the ball.

In disagreements, asking "What's a fair solution ?" can be a good way to resolve them.

From the author and illustrator. Thank you for your purchase.

I hope you and the young people in your life you share Little Lessons, Wisdom & Truth Volume I with enjoy the read and take something positive and constructive away from the stories.

If you like the book, please direct others to where you found it or to **LIBBLLC.WEEBLY.COM/BOOKS.HTML**.

If you have feedback, suggestions or lessons you'd like to see in future volumes please forward them to **LLWTBOOK@GMAIL.COM**. Thank you again.

Take a picture of the website link or tear off / cut out tags to make it easy to locate the book.

Little Lessons, Wisdom & Truth Volume I by Baba Ganoush

LIBBLLC.WEEBLY.COM/BOOKS.HTML

Little Lessons, Wisdom & Truth Volume I by Baba Ganoush

LIBBLLC.WEEBLY.COM/BOOKS.HTML

Little Lessons, Wisdom & Truth Volume I by Baba Ganoush

LIBBLLC.WEEBLY.COM/BOOKS.HTML

Made in the USA
Columbia, SC
30 October 2018